A BASKET
FULL OF FIGS

Green Bean Books

First published in the UK in 2020
by Green Bean Books

c/o Pen & Sword Books Ltd
47 Church Street, Barnsley, S. Yorkshire, S70 2AS
www.greenbeanbooks.com

Text © Ori Elon, 2017
Illustrations © Menahem Halberstadt, 2017
English edition © Green Bean Books, 2020
English language translation © Harold Grinspoon Foundation

Paperback edition: 978-1-78438-472-2
Harold Grinspoon Foundation edition: 978-1-78438-476-0

Designed by Tina Garcia
Edited by Kate Baker, Claire Berliner, Julie Carpenter and Phoebe Jascourt
Production by Hugh Allan

Printed in China by Imago
012028.6K1/B1468/A6

FSC
www.fsc.org

MIX
Paper from
responsible sources
FSC® C005748

A BASKET
FULL OF FIGS

Retold by Ori Elon, according to the Midrash

Illustrated by Menahem Halberstadt

Translated by Gilah Kahn-Hoffmann

In a quiet little village, the local people are hiding inside their houses, peering through the windows in awe.

"Here he comes," they whisper nervously.

Along the main street, astride his great horse, the mighty Emperor Hadrian comes riding in.

Still hiding and peering,
the villagers watch as a door opens
and an old man carrying a hoe
steps into his garden.

The emperor brings
his great horse to a halt.
"What are you doing?" he asks.
"I'm digging a small hole
to plant a small fig tree,"
replies the old man cheerfully.

"A fig tree? But how old are you?"
asks the curious emperor.
The old man finishes digging
and leans on his hoe.
"In exactly two weeks," he says proudly,
"I will be one hundred years old."

He gently places the fig
sapling into the hole.
He covers its roots with damp soil,
pats it down, and waters it.
The emperor is astonished.
"But the tree is so small,"
he says, "and you are so old!
Surely you won't live
long enough to eat its fruit?!"
The old man smiles and replies,
"Well, if I don't,
then my children will."

"The tree that I am planting
is a gift. For years to come,
children will visit this
place and find a fig tree
full of sweet fruit."
The old man looks around at
his village fondly and continues.
"After all, when I came into this world,
one hundred years ago,
there were lots of trees here.
There were fig, pomegranate, mulberry
and date trees, all offering
cool shade and delicious fruit –
wonderful gifts
that earlier generations
had kindly left for me."

The old man finishes
planting his tree and
Emperor Hadrian rides on.
One year passes.
Then another.
And then another.

After three long years,
the emperor returns to the village.
Just as before, all the people
are hiding inside their houses, peering
through the windows in awe.
"Here he comes," they
whisper nervously.

Along the main street,
astride his great horse,
the mighty Emperor Hadrian
comes riding in.

Still hiding and peering, the villagers
watch as a door opens and an old man
carrying a basket steps into his garden.

The emperor brings
his great horse to a halt.
"What are you doing?" he asks.
"Don't you remember?"
replies the old man cheerfully.

"I'm the old man you met here
three years ago. Here is the tree
that I planted, and look –
here, in my basket, are the figs."

"I have lived long enough to eat the fruit,
and my children and grandchildren
now enjoy them, too.
Please, Your Majesty,
come down off your horse
and try them for yourself!"

Remembering the old man and his tree, the emperor smiles.
He climbs down from his horse and bites into a fig.
He eats one.
Then another.
And then another.

Content at last, and with a belly full of figs,
the Emperor Hadrian hands the basket to the old man,
then climbs onto his horse.
"Of all the figs I have ever tasted,"
he exclaims, "these are by far the sweetest!"

The old man peers into the basket.
But instead of figs, it is full to the brim with gold!

The emperor rides on.
And the old man, who was once a small boy
resting in this very spot,
lies in the shade of the fig tree.
He looks at the trees all around him and
sees so many gifts, one after another, after another.

He sees fig trees, almond trees,
jasmine trees, and lemon trees.
He sees pomegranates, olives, mulberries, and carobs.
A peach tree, an oak tree,
a date palm, a cypress, and a grapevine.

Old trees and new trees, all offering
cool shade and delicious fruit.
So many gifts for so many children,
today and for generations to come.

Ori Elon, author

Ori Elon is a critically acclaimed Israeli filmmaker and writer. He is the co-creator of the television drama *Shtisel,* which won 17 Israeli Academy Awards, and the author of *The Invisible Show,* winner of the Israeli Ministry of Culture Best Novel award. His children's books include *King Gogle* and *In the Z'akrobat Market.*

Menahem Halberstadt, illustrator

Menahem Halberstadt is an illustrator of children's books, magazines, and newspapers. He has illustrated several books for major publishing houses in Israel, and his work has been exhibited in various shows, including a solo exhibition at the Jerusalem Illustration Festival.

Green
Bean
Books

Other Green Bean Books

SIGNS in the WELL

Written by Shoham Smith
Illustrations by Vali Mintzi

Signs in the Well

Written by Shoham Smith

Illustrated by Vali Mintzi

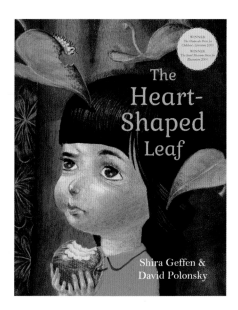

The Heart-Shaped Leaf

Written by Shira Geffen

Illustrated by David Polonsky

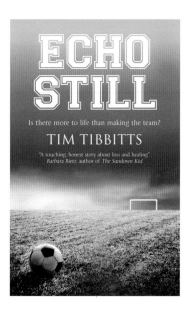

Echo Still

Written by Tim Tibbitts

The Sages of Chelm and the Moon

Written by Shlomo Abas

Illustrated by Omer Hoffmann

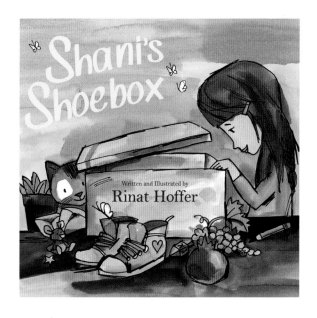

Shani's Shoebox

Written and illustrated

by Rinat Hoffer